The Pearl

Dignity Press
World Dignity University Press

Arctic Queen (www.arctic-queen.com) is the artist name of Ragnhild Nilsen, one of Scandinavia`s greatest public speakers and inspirators. Besides being a gifted storyteller, singer and composer, she is the author of 14 books – both poetic novels and more practical books about leadership, presentation skills and change management.

Arctic Queen spends much of her time on the ecological cotton revolution, an initiative she has taken together with SEKEM on behalf of global warming and fair trade. See more at www.globalfairtrade.com and www.sekemscandinavia.com.

Arctic Queen

The Pearl

A poetic story about finding your talents
and using them

Translated from Norwegian into English
by Sean Kinsella

Dignity Press
World Dignity University Press

Published by Dignity Press
16 Northview Court
Lake Oswego, OR 97035, USA
http://www.dignitypress.org
Ref. # 11030

Book design by Uli Spalthoff
Cover graphics by Diane Cutler
More about this book at www.dignitypress.org/the-pearl

Printed on paper from environmentally managed forestry. See
www.lightningsource.com/chainofcustody for certifications.

ISBN 978-1-937570-00-2
Also available as eBook (ISBN 978-1-937570-06-4)

To Mischa

Contents

Prologue

The high, rugged mountain looked down upon the boat that set out from the beach with the two lovers onboard. It let its shadow fall over the waves and sighed sadly: "Now those two are leaving with high hopes for a new beginning. Such a thing could never happen to me."

The mountain howled its lament to the sky. "Oh, I'm so tired of being stuck," it groaned. "This is my fate, in the same place day in and day out. How is it going to end? Can anyone set me free?"

That evening, a cloud sailed towards the mountain. It had planned to ascend beyond the mountain formation, as it usually did. But on this particular night, the cloud took a turn into a gorge, and as it gently rubbed itself into the massif, it heard some kind of sigh or groan: "Aw, aw."

"Are you talking to me?" asked the cloud.

The mountain was lightly disconcerted that someone had bothered to listen, and was silent for a moment, but as it was so used to its own lament, it soon began to groan again. The cloud was just about to get underway but on hearing the sigh from the mountain, decided to stay for the night. In complete silence, it wrapped itself around the mountain's heart like a light blanket.

"Talk to me," it whispered. "I am here."

"I'm so heavy," said the mountain. "I can't go anywhere. I stand here, day after day in the same spot. I feel unfulfilled."

"Yes, that must be awful," said the cloud. "Life itself is all about movement and flow."

"Indeed," said the mountain and felt even more insignificant.

The cloud rubbed against the mountaintop and gently caressed its neck.

"Can I tell you a secret?"

"Of course," said the mountain. "Now that I've told you mine, you might as well."

"Sometimes, I feel too light," said the cloud.

"What do you mean?" asked the mountain.

The cloud settled itself into the mountain and said in a barely audible whisper: "You see. I disappear and I can't find myself again."

"Hmm," said the mountain, "I never thought about that being a problem."

The cloud began to weep and the mountain pulled it closer.

"Rest awhile here with me. Right here, right now with me, you exist," it said. "If you want you can tell me a bit about your travels. But if you'd rather be silent, then that's alright too."

And this is how the mountain and the cloud became sweethearts. That night they made love for the first time. The next morning, when the cloud had cleared, the mountain discovered something it had left behind, a memento of their sweet meeting: a shiny pearl was born in a mountain stream that morning.

And ever since then, both the mountain and the cloud have known that they need each other to find themselves and enjoy their particular talents.

And we humans can adorn ourselves with this insight.

Part 1

When an old tree gives shelter to the
tired wanderer, a pearl is born.

1

The young woman had walked far when she came to the village by the sea. A storm was brewing. She was tired and she stopped at a few houses to ask for shelter through the night. But no one had a room to offer a strange woman who roamed on her own in the dark. She looked around for a place to rest and caught sight of a crooked old apple tree that stood by the roadside. She lay down in the shelter of its branches and, quite exhausted, soon fell asleep to the sound of the violent gusts of wind and the beating of the waves upon the beach. The woman's name was Mara.

Suddenly she awoke.

The storm had passed. It was in the middle of the night. A reflection of the moon shimmered upon the sea's swaths of silver and only a few ripples remained, to hint at what had gone before. Mara inhaled the scent of apple blossoms and she saw like a crack in the night sky how the white blossoms reached for the moon.

There lay a mussel right at her feet.

The storm must have thrown it up from the depths of the ocean and now the moonlight kissed it tenderly - coaxing it to open. The mussel's pure pearl slowly revealed itself. Overwhelmed by the magic of the moon, the beauty of the pearl and the scent of the apple blossoms, Mara sat up and began to sing out towards the sea. Her clear voice mingled with the sound of the rhythmic dance of the waves upon the beach. She sang of longing and hope. She gave voice to desires and dreams for her future. The sea listened. And then, like an echo from a deep, melancholic voice, it sang back to her: "Be patient my child. Ask and you shall receive. Seek and you shall find. Knock and soon the door will be opened for you."

All at once she sensed that she was no longer alone.

In the light of the moon she could see that the whole beach was filled with mussels that opened up to reveal their secret treasures. Mara got to her feet. She took a deep breath and bowed her head low and with reverence in the direction from which she had come. Then, turning to the crooked old apple tree, she said: "Because the people of the village were kind enough to reject me, I now find myself under your blessed apple blossoms – surrounded by mussels and pearls.

M ara skipped along the beach and collected some of the mussels. One by one she gathered them in her apron. Very carefully she took out their beautiful pearls and put them into a little cloth pouch in which she used to carry small change. The pearls lent the pouch a distinctive weight as it hung there from the leather belt she had fastened around her waist.

The teasing rays of the morning sun brought the village gradually to life. Some set about their daily business. Others got to work on checking what kind of damage the storm had inflicted on houses and huts. Few noticed the solitary figure of the woman who wandered up from the beach. A couple of fishermen nodded to her but they were too busy examining their nets and checking how their boats had fared in the storm to really register her presence.

Hunger gnawed at her stomach. The sweet smell from the bakery down the street was enough to attract people in droves. She stepped across the threshold and began to sniff at all the delicious aromas of cinnamon and vanilla and freshly baked bread and buns. When the women from the village had been served, she approached the counter.

"Two buns and a loaf of bread, please!"

The baker put her order on the counter and told her the price.

Mara laid three gleaming white pearls on the counter. The baker was a plump and pleasant man and he could see by the woman's eyes that she was very hungry. But he had mouths to feed himself and he was skeptical to the idea of exchanging bread for pearls. What if they turned out to be fakes!

"I'll give you the buns and the bread for the three pearls this time," he said, "but you go to the jeweller just down the street and he'll help you find out what these pearls are worth."

Mara munched greedily on the buns as she plodded down the street. What should she tell the jeweller? Should she say that she'd found the pearls on the beach? Would it be better to say that she'd inherited them from her mother? Should she show him the whole pouch? What if the jeweller was a ruthless type and tried to deceive her?

She found a little hiding place behind a cart, sat down and divided the pearls into two piles in front of her. She put one pile in the cloth pouch and fastened it to her belt. She put the other pile in her bag under some clothes.

A pleasant ring came from the little bell above the door as Mara entered the jeweller's shop. Jewellery shone alluringly on all the different shelves. Single pearls lay like beautiful drops in glittering gold rings and gilded bracelets. She gently stroked the pouch of pearls she carried on her belt and smiled hesitantly to the elderly man who stood with an air of authority behind the counter. There was a a pince-nez hanging by a string down on his big stomach.

"I found these pearls on a beach," she said and put the pouch on the counter, her face flushed. "Are they of any value?"

The jeweller spread the pearls out upon a green cloth, brought his pince-nez slowly up his face and studied the pearls one by one while he held them up to the light. Eventually he glanced over at her again.

"Deep sea pearls," he nodded and caught her eye. "Some of them are rare in these parts."

Mara looked down; how could the pearls possibly be rare?

"This black pearl is very beautiful," he said, "where did you get it?"

Mara wanted to tell him the truth; that it had lain hidden in a mussel under an old apple tree, but felt that the actual memory was too precious to her to just give it away to a stranger. She held her arms around herself:

"Unfortunately I...can't tell you that," she said, "but I'd very much like to know what these pearls are worth and if they can be of use."

"Well...it all depends of course," said the jeweller and frowned. "This pearl here has a little dent in it. That reduces its value immediately! And this little white one here is just too small to fit on a pearl necklace."

He removed his pince-nez and looked up:

"Shall we say three gold pieces for thirty-seven pearls?"

Mara didn't know if this was a good price. Right there and then she was only conscious of what her stomach was telling her: "I'm hungry and you can buy food with that money." She agreed to the sum offered.

Now she had gold coins in the little pouch that slapped lightly against her hip. She felt a blissful sensation well up in her chest that hadn't been there before. Mara wondered how the jeweller could say that the pearls were rare when she'd found them on a beach right beside the very village he lived in. Mara decided to ask some fishermen if they ever came across pearls on the beach. She approached a group of them who sat repairing their nets after the storm. She spoke to several of them but they all shook their heads. None of them had ever found pearls on the beach but yes, once in a while they were lucky enough to come across a couple of pearls in the mussels which got caught in the nets.

"But," said one fisherman, a tall, thin man with big hands, "there's a pearl diver in our village. Go ask him."

With that, all the fishermen laughed.

At the end of the long beach, Mara eventually found the pearl diver's cottage. It looked deserted. She cleared her throat noisily and when that didn't work she called out. But no one appeared. She touched the door gently. It swung open and she looked inside. The cottage was small and simply furnished: a table, a couple of chairs and a bed, which was made up and had a beautifully patterned blue bedspread on it. A couple of saucepans and some mugs hung on the wall, as did a casting net and a landing net.

Mara closed the door, put down her bag outside the cottage, leaned against the wall and looked out over the ocean that shimmered playfully in the sun. She wanted to wait for the pearl diver to come back. But the sun drifted majestically across the sky and still no pearl diver showed up.

There was a simple meal prepared in the cottage on the beach that evening. Mara ate it alone. She was tired and lay down under the bedspread. Not long after, she fell asleep to the gentle song of the waves on the beach.

2

The next day, Mara went to the market square to buy fresh vegetables, fruit and spices. She wanted to take them back to the pearl diver's cottage as a gesture of goodwill. No matter whom she asked she couldn't find out where the pearl diver was to be found. Some shrugged their shoulders indifferently when she asked; whilst others said that the pearl diver was in the habit of travelling. Yes, he'd be gone a good while – then suddenly he'd show up again. The last time he went off they hadn't seen him for a couple of years.

What if she could stay at his cottage?

No one could give her permission to stay, but with the jeweller's and the baker's consent she moved in. Mara washed and cleaned the cottage, hung up spices and herbs to dry and picked flowers which she placed in pots by the door. She sewed a blouse for herself out of a length of beautiful red fabric and stitched a new pouch to hold the pearls. She hid the pouch under the mattress.

People began to nod in acknowledgement to this young woman who had shown up amongst them out of the blue, and the jeweller asked her if she would serve as his apprentice. For one thing, there was something about this strange woman that he liked and for another, perhaps some more of those pearls might turn up.

Thus it came to pass that Mara became a jeweller's apprentice.

By day she worked at setting the pearls into moulds and at night she slept in the pearl diver's cottage. But on nights when the moon was full and a storm howled, and everyone in the village was safe behind locked doors and boarded up windows, she made her way back to the old apple tree, buried her hands in the sand and sang her songs of yearning to the sea.

On nights like this, painful memories rose to the surface. Mara remembered what she had left behind – and the pain returned. She realized she could easily loose herself in the past, embellish it or let it be. At times she attempted to hold onto the pain so she wouldn't forget who she was and what she had been through. But the security of daily life in the village and the peaceful nights in the pearl diver's cottage gradually began to have an effect on her. The bad memories faded – yes, they assumed a grey tone; grew hazy and disappeared into a kind of mist. The hurt, the pain, even the wrath and evil of mankind could only be called to mind if she made an effort to do so. Often the images dissolved and drifted into recollections of intimacy and warmth from when she was a little girl – memories of lullabies her mother sang and of stories at bedtime or the afternoons her father took her out to the stable and they went on long horse rides together.

In time, what Mara remembered best were the good, wholesome days and moments of joy. It surprised her, but she gradually began to smile more.

At daybreak, when the storm had abated, she gathered the mussels and carried them in her apron – just like the first time. Mara often wondered why no one else in the village knew about this secret. After a while she had enough pearls in the cottage to fill seven pouches full of them. All of which lay well concealed under the mattress. She could feel them under her feet when she lay in bed at night.

Time went by. Mara was pleased that she could use her pearls and the jeweller was very pleased with the work she did. She not only possessed the dexterity required of a good jeweller, she was also gifted with imagination. The jeweller thought her gift ought to be developed in order to give old, beautiful pieces new life, as he told her.

All the same, now and again she was troubled by a strange nagging thought that led to a feeling of restlessness in her soul: "Is this really what I want to do for work? Setting my pearls in gold and fashioning them into beautified shapes to adorn rich ladies?" There were days when her restlessness welled up inside her so much so that she would stop in the middle of her work and gaze longingly out over the sea. But the jeweller was a pleasant fellow.

She had a job to go to. She had enough money to buy all the pastries her heart desired, and she'd become friendly with other young women from around the area. They told her lively tales about the fun to be had in the evenings. Together they giggled at the hopeless boys in the village or they flirted their way to romantic rendezvous. Mara was no longer a stranger. The village had warmed to her and she to it. She brushed the troubling thoughts aside and got on with the business of her everyday life in which one day melted into the next.

I n the nights when her anxiety couldn't be assuaged, she would sometimes write in a little, brown notebook she had found in a drawer under the dining table in the pearl diver's cottage. The first time she discovered this notebook she had let out a slight gasp – had the pearl diver written down anything about his life? But the book was empty, filled with blank sheets. There were a couple of pencils in the drawer. On an impulse, Mara lit the oil lamp on the little table, turned to the first blank page and wrote:

> If you find a pearl,
> take good care of it.

She smiled at the sentence that had taken shape on the blank sheet of paper and continued:

If the pearl is small,
listen to the song from its pure heart.

Eagerly she wrote down the little insights that took shape:

Pearls have their own melody.

Those who look for a pearl every day find happy moments.

If you think the pearl is too far out of your reach then take a closer look at your heart, you'll be surprised by what you find.

Mara let out a sigh of satisfaction, looked around the little room and let her eyes linger awhile on the familiar objects there: the fishing net by the door, the pot of little wildflowers and the blue bedspread. Then she leaned over the book and added a question:

Which pearls lie hidden in your story?

Something tightened in her stomach. Who can talk about pearls when there are so many painful memories? No sound passed her lips. Instead she heard a weak knock on the door, almost like a couple of clicks. She got up from the chair and took a look outside.

Had she been mistaken about the knocking sound? She sat back down at the table in order to immerse herself further in the pearl issue. There was another knock at the door. This time she ran to the door and flung it open. She stood in the doorway, and there, like a silhouette drawn by the moon, she could make out a figure down by the shore. Was it a man or a beast?

Mara walked slowly down towards the figure. She had heard tales of mermaids, and now she sensed that such a woman had blessed her with a visit. The figure had small breasts and long beautiful hair matted with kelp and sea tangle. Around her neck she wore a large gleaming white mussel. From her waist down she was clothed in a sort of greenish-blue dress – no, it was fish scales which covered her thighs and feet.

"Did you knock on my door?"

The mermaid motioned for her to sit down beside her on the beach.

"I'd like to give you this mussel," she said, in a strange, soft voice. It sounded more like she sang rather than spoke as she stole a glance up at Mara with her big innocent eyes.

"I understand you collect mussels?"

Mara took the bluish black mussel the mermaid gave her. She invited the mermaid into the cottage, but the amphibious woman shook her head firmly.

"I can't move too well on the beach, so I threw pebbles at your door in order to get you to come to me."

Mara stroked the mussel she'd been given.

"I only want to ask you something before I glide out into the depths of the sea again," sang the mermaid. "What do you do with all the mussels you find on the beach?"

"I crack them open, sell the pearls to the jeweller and place them into jewelry."

The mermaid tossed her beautiful head for a moment, and held tightly to the large white mussel hanging around her neck.

"We wear the mussels unopened around our necks to remind us of its wisdom."

The mermaid flapped her tail ever so gently. "Do you know the story?"

Mara shook her head. The amphibious woman emitted a few bubbles of air to signal that she must soon return to the deep:

"Once, a long time ago, a beautiful mussel got a grain of sand lodged in its tissue. The mussel attempted to get rid of the sand for a long time, but no matter what it did, the grain of sand stuck to it and worked its way deeper into the tissue. It was painful. After repeated attempts to remove the grain of sand, the mussel decided to try something different. It began to spin mother-of-pearl around the grain. Gradually the scar healed and the grain of sand changed into a unique pearl."

The mermaid sighed and caressed the mussel which hung from her neck. "That's how the mussels taught my people that scars and wounds can become the most beautiful pearls."

"That was a beautiful story," said Mara as she looked over this fantastic creature who sat right in front of her. The mermaid smelled of sea and sand and seemed so full of vigour. She then began to wriggle and crawl back into the water.

"Before you go, honourable mermaid, can I ask you a question?"

The mermaid stopped up for a moment and glanced at Mara.

"Do you think that I should stop opening mussels and taking the pearls out of them?"

"You must do as you wish, dear human child. What's important to keep in mind is this: pick only one pearl every day."

"What do you mean?"

"To take notice of a special pearl every day helps you to open your eyes. To find one pearl every day serves to show you what is important in your life".

And with that, the mermaid disappeared out into the waves.

3

One day as Mara worked in the jewellers shop, setting one of her most beautiful white pearls as the centre point between two red rubies in a gold ring, she thought she heard the pearl whisper something to her. It said: "I am a dream. For far too long I've lain hidden in the depths of the ocean. Let me become real!"

She marvelled at what she thought she'd heard. When the ring with the two rubies and the pearl was finished, she wrote a little note which she put into the box alongside the ring: "*Two hearts and one dream*".

She was just putting the finishing touches on a brooch she had shaped like a rose when a man came into the jeweller's shop. Mara glanced up from her work as she heard the little bell over the door tinkle and nodded to the stranger.

"I'm looking for a pearl necklace," he said.

Mara showed him different necklaces with pearls in rows of twos and threes, but the man shook his head and looked around the shop impassively. Then he saw the brooch she had just finished working on.

"What's that?"

"A brooch. It could adorn a beautiful dress or be used to fasten a shawl."

She took out the golden brooch she had fashioned like a rose. In the very centre there lay a small shimmering pearl. The man gazed at the piece pensively for a while.

"My wife doesn't think she's good enough," he said, while he stroked the brooch gently. "Even though she's the most wonderful woman to be found, she doesn't think her talents are up to much."

He bit his lower lip.

"I so much want to give her a piece of jewellery that can serve to remind her how beautiful and talented she is in my eyes."

"Then this pearl has found its meaning and its person."

Mara put the brooch into the man's hand.

"This piece is called '*Courage of the Rose*'. And this is what the pearl said to me as I pondered where to place it in the mould: "*I may be small, but I have the strength of a rose.*"

That night Mara lit the oil lamp in the pearl diver's cottage, sat down at the little table and took out the notebook. Her thoughts flowed easily and were committed to paper:

*You create your own dreams and transform
them into pearls.*

Every dream is spun from mother-of-pearl

*A moment is a bright spot in your existence;
a shimmering pearl in the tapestry of your
life.*

*When you find a pearl, it's up to you to
decide the importance it shall have in your
life.*

*Every day is a pearl dive; a new opportunity
to find the mussel's wisdom.*

She stopped to listen for a moment. Had there been a knock at the door again tonight? No, it was probably just the wind whistling around the cottage. She continued writing pensively:

Do you wish to become a pearl diver?

*A pearl diver finds pearls where others forget
to look.*

There was a knock at the door. Mara was sure of it. She opened the door and peeped out. Out in the foamy surf a dolphin was jumping. It moved quickly, and dived under the waves before she could say hello. When it emerged again, it shouted to the woman on the beach:

"Come on in."

"Now's not a good time."

"Then when?"

"I've got a lot to do."

"Have you forgotten how to play, little human child?"

Mara decided to take the plunge. She undressed and left her clothes on the beach before she threw herself naked out into the waves. Breathe out. Breathe in. Her swimming strokes directed the rhythm until she let herself be carried away by the intense flirt of the dolphin. She grabbed its fin and howled with joy as it pulled her through the water with a speed and intensity she had never experienced before. Its eagerness was infectious. An intense tickling in her stomach gave way to a powerful, bubbling energy, and she heard the dolphin cackle:

"A journey of a thousand miles begins with a single stroke!"

When she finally let go and turned over onto her back to rest in the smooth surface of the sea beyond the surf, the dolphin glided over to her side.

"How do you manage to retain such passion?" she asked.

The dolphin laughed. "Ah, you people are strange. You understand so little. You all sail out in your little boats and ships, with such purpose, such sobriety. You forget to play."

"Most children play in the waves," insisted Mara.

"And what happens when they grow up?"

The dolphin rocked gently to and fro, as if to indicate a little impatience.

"I suppose by that stage they've played themselves out," she said, feeling slightly foolish as soon as she'd uttered the words.

"Poor things," chattered the dolphin, as it laid its head a little to the side and looked at her with blinking eyes. "Do you know the dolphin's recipe for success?"

"No, what is it?"

"Swim towards that good feeling and the rest will fall into place!"

"But you can't play your way to success?"

"You can't?"

The dolphin performed a lively pirouette in front of her: "What kind of feelings do you get when you play?"

"Inner joy and delight!"

"Would you like to experience those feelings every day?"

Mara felt the fluid levity that the water gave her. Would she dare feel this good every day? What about the pain that reminded her of who she was and where she came from? Could she allow herself to let go of that?

"Swim after the sincere fluid delight in all your moments, and you'll fulfil your dreams before you know it," the dolphin cheered and disappeared beneath the waves with ardour.

She swam with slow strokes towards the beach before she stretched out and surfed through the breakwater.

The flirt with the dolphin had made Mara feel warm and happy. She lay awhile in the water's edge and let the waves caress her naked body.

Part 2

When a butterfly's wing
calms the mighty storm,
a pearl is born.

One day a merchant came to the little village by the sea. He was delivering some goods to the jeweller and after they'd finished their business, the two men sat down by the counter and had a chat over a drink. While they sat there and let their minds wander, the merchant caught sight of a woman who was picking flowers on the other side of the jeweller's garden fence. There was something in the way she moved and especially in how she drew the loose strands of golden hair away from her forehead that made him study her even more closely.

Shortly after, the merchant was leaning over the fence doing his best to act in a casual manner.

"Beautiful flowers," he said.

Mara looked up and smiled at him.

That was how they met.

He was a hardworking businessman, who travelled a great deal, but now he visited her as often as he could. He told Mara about the big city he came from, about his beautiful house, about everything she could do and see if she married him. Mara was happy in the village by the sea and she was beginning to develop quite a reputation for her beautiful pearl inlaid rings and trinkets. All the same, there was something in her that spurred her to move on. The jeweller tried to convince her to stay, but when he understood that it was no use he said in a paternal way: "When you become a housewife, don't forget your talents."

They had a big wedding. Mara brought her wedding chest with her and followed her husband to his house, his family and his city – as was the tradition. She was both anxious and excited when she stepped into the big house. According to her husband, now that she was married, it wasn't necessary for her to work anymore. He'd provide the means for them to live. She didn't have to worry about anything like that.

Mara loved her husband and did as he and others expected of her. After the honeymoon, daily life set in and she spent her time decorating the house. After a while she made friends who had more expensive tastes in clothes and all things fashion than she was used to. She gabbled and jabbered on subjects both important and trivial. She acquired a taste for fine materials and elaborately woven pieces and she frequented colourful markets where pots and pans, carpets and textiles could be found.

After a while she became pregnant. As the child in her belly grew, Mara began to weave. Where before she'd used her pearls to make jewellery, she now began to set pearls as signs and symbols of good things to come into the tapestries she wove. "Imagination is just as important as knowledge," she thought to herself, as she sat for hours by the loom and let ancient myths and beautiful tales give rhythm to the warp.

She gave birth to a little girl. Mara finally felt infinitely blessed when the child came. They named her Helen, which means "the bright one". She inherited her mother's radiant beauty and her father's raven hair. Now she had everything she wanted: a child, a husband she loved and a beautiful house. What more could she ask for?

The days turned into months, and the months into years, and the years came and went. The yearly rhythms were transformed into beautiful tapestries; the brittle colours of autumn dissolved into the wild exuberant fireworks of summer. Then autumn came and the tapestries changed in radiance and content, before the rhythmic strokes of the shuttle laid winter's long, white stories in the warp. Mara felt like the loom had become her second home and the pictures she created the language of her soul. The jeweller had once shown her a path to explore. Now she trod that path. Although the imprint she left was another, it was created with the same intensity and earnest desire to affect others. Often she would weave exquisite, rare pearls into her tapestries.

People who came to visit admired her tapestries and some stood gazing at them for long hours. After a while they discovered the different stories and fantastic little tales which lay hidden in them, not to mention all the different pearls that animated and fuelled the stories the tapestries told. Some people were so moved by the tapestries that their eyes filled with tears. Others simply abandoned whatever everyday conversation they were engaged in and sat in silence in front of a tapestry. It wasn't rare for visitors to ask how she managed to weave tapestries like this that spoke to their very souls.

"The tapestries weave themselves," she would answer. "I am their loving servant."

Her husband saw how Mara's artistic talent developed and it struck him that there was a profit to be made here. Being a businessman, he could see that the tapestries his wife made could be sold for a tidy sum. But when he mentioned this to her, she shook her head in horror and said: "The tapestries I weave belong to the language of my soul. I cannot sell my heart."

He thought her words peculiar – there were a lot of things that were peculiar about this woman he'd married. She was near but at the same time distant, as if she longed for a place where he couldn't go. When all was said and done, he thought it was unnecessary for her to use so much time working on something that wasn't rational and which couldn't be sold either. His attitude hurt Mara's feelings so she tried to behave like other women and dedicate herself to the needs of their child, to practical tasks and to outings with her friends. She only worked on her pictures and tapestries in secret now, preferably when her husband wasn't at home, or at night while he slept.

She had left the brown notebook at the pearl diver's cottage, as a surprise for him, should he ever show up. Yet some nights she still wrote down the thoughts that came to her as she sat and weaved. Lately she had sensed this insight:

> When a tear comes to water your
> yearning, a pearl is born.

2

When little Helen was about five years old she got the measles. Her mother nursed her, cooled her brow with damp cloths and sat by the bedside telling her stories. The child loved to listen to these, especially the one about the mermaid. Mara had to tell her again and again how mermaids leave the pearl in the mussel and drape them around their necks as jewellery.

"Mother, what does it mean that a scar can create a pearl?"

"It means that what was once painful can heal and become a secret treasure."

That night the child's fever rose and the next day little Helen died. The infection had spread to the brain and Mara lost the most precious thing she had given life to.

With the loss of the child, her husband's heart hardened. Instead of letting the pain become a river he could sail on together with his wife, he shut her out. One painful thought seized upon the other and his mind began to fill with worry. He was used to worrying from before – those who run their own business know what it is to be anxious. But now another kind of worry took hold of him: concern for what his wife was up to when he wasn't at home, and when she claimed to be sitting weaving. Gradually suspicion took up the bulk of his waking thoughts. He said to himself: "What if my wife is unfaithful when I'm away?"

Mara missed her daughter. Her complexion drained of colour and her face became grey and narrow. There was no laughter to be heard in the big house anymore. She sealed her sorrow inside but she did not leave her husband's side. At all social gatherings, where they were amongst his many friends and business associates, she continued to be present and to support him in her gentle, mournful manner.

Even though he appreciated her support, her husband couldn't manage to keep the painful thoughts at bay. After a while he noticed that his wife was often particularly considerate towards him right before he set out on long business trips. He thought there must be some reason for it so he began to come home earlier than announced, in order to keep up with what she was doing when he wasn't at home, only to discover that she either lay sleeping peacefully in their bed or that she was sitting alone at the loom. Once when he came home unexpectedly, he saw there were tears running down her cheeks and his eyes fell upon a note which lay on the ground beside the loom:

When a rainbow kisses the earth, a pearl is born.

What sort of a waste of time and energy was this!?

One night he crept into the house like a thief and discovered that his wife lay naked in bed. He had never known her to do that when he was away and so he instantly became gripped by a jealous rage. He was sure she had a lover hiding somewhere. Instead of asking, he threw himself over her and that night they made love with a passion that they had rarely experienced before. The next week he found her naked in bed again. But not only that, this time the bed was covered in beautiful, fragrant petals and she had a wreath of wildflowers in her hair. In her hand she held a little card with the words:

When you embrace your tears and let them nurture your soul, a pearl is born.

"Who has she done all this for?" he thought and he went to wake her. But she seemed in such a deep sleep and looked so peaceful that he refrained. Instead he lay down beside her and dwelt upon sad thoughts of who she had been with before he had gotten home and to whom she had written those words.

Thus it went on for months until he couldn't bear to touch his wife anymore as he was sure she had a lover. He thought it embarrassing and humiliating to tell her what sorts of thoughts he battled with, so he decided to keep his mouth shut. But he was sure that she was hiding something.

3

The next time he was due to embark on a long business trip he led her to think he would be away for a lot longer than he actually intended to be. His plan was to come home as early as the next night to see whom she was with. And sure enough, as he crept into the house the following night, he thought he could discern the sound of low moaning coming from upstairs in the bedroom. He raced up the stairs and found his wife in the act of changing the bedclothes. She smiled in surprise as her husband rushed into the bedroom.

"I couldn't sleep," she said, "so I thought I may as well put some clean sheets on the bed."

Only then did her husband's eyes fall upon the big chest that his wife had brought with her when they married. It stood at the end of the bed but he'd never bothered to find out what was in it. On this particular night he got it into his head that his wife's lover was hiding in the wedding chest.

"You're lying," he cried, "You have a lover! And he's hiding in that big chest."

Mara slumped down on the top of the chest and sat gaping at him.

"How could you think such a thing of me?" she groaned.

"Out of the way, woman," he said and made to push her off. "I'm going to throttle him."

"Don't say such things, darling."

She wouldn't budge.

"Move!"

Mara refused to get up. Then her husband said, in barely concealed triumph:

"If you won't move, then this chest is going into the ground! We'll bury it together tonight!"

After a lot of yelling and screaming, she agreed.

They took the chest out into the garden. It was heavy but despite the difficulty they managed to drag it out. Her husband found a spade, dug a large hole and then they lowered it into the ground before they threw stones and earth on top and covered it up.

Three months passed.

Mara grew more and more unhappy. Her husband was aware of this, but he was stubborn and angry. "That's the punishment for adultery," he thought.

After a while however, he felt it was time to put the arguments and strife behind them, but no matter how much effort he put in to try and improve her humour, he couldn't manage to make his wife happy again. She glared at him in the mornings and she wouldn't talk to him in the evenings. One night she refused to lie beside him in their bed and shortly after that had practically moved out of their bedroom altogether. Her husband despaired. He had no idea what to do to win his wife back. At the same time, he didn't want to give in because he believed it was her fault that they'd landed in this situation and that it was she who should come to him, fall on her knees and beg for forgiveness.

One night, while he lay there alone in bed unable to sleep, he decided to dig up the chest and look at the remains of the lover she had once had. He was willing to go to the police, turn in himself and his wife and plead guilty to the murder of her lover. They could receive their punishment – each in their own way – if need be. Fair was fair.

He went out, got the spade and started to dig. After a while he found the chest. He brushed away the stones and loose earth and, slowly opening the lid, prepared himself for the gruesome sight within. But what he saw was very different from what he had expected. Even in his wildest dreams he couldn't have prepared himself for this: the chest was filled with beautiful woven pictures strewn with pearls! Some of Helen's clothes lay as colourful mementoes between the tapestries and he counted seven red cloth pouches full of the biggest pearls he'd ever seen.

Wide-eyed, he looked up from the pit and realised his wife had come down to the garden. He could just make her out in the dim moonlight that shone upon the grass. He could see she was naked.

Mara came slowly closer. She was singing or humming a peculiar melody. It was both frightening and magical at the same time. He stood there spell-bound, with the spade in his hand. When she finally came to the edge of the hole he was standing in, she threw neither stones nor earth at him. The melody she'd been singing ceased. Instead she said: "Keep as many pearls as you want. Perhaps one day they'll help you climb out of that hole you've dug for yourself."

Part 3

When a rainbow kisses the
longing earth, a pearl is born.

1

The woman had travelled far when she came to the village by the sea. The beautiful clothes she wore were dusty, dirty and wet. Her long hair was unkempt. She knocked on the baker's door. He gasped when he realised who it was and took her inside. A fire was lit and a table lain with bread and cakes. While her wet clothes hung to dry, Mara sat wrapped up in a lovely, soft blanket and they reminisced about the good old days and common acquaintances. Then he asked the inevitable question of what had brought her back to these parts.

"I'm just passing through," she said, and wiped her brow. She knew she looked tired. "I'm on my way up to a village in the mountains I've heard about in order to settle down there."

Mara told about the child she had lost and about her broken marriage.

"I've come here because I need to spend a little time in the pearl diver's old cottage, then I'll be on my way."

"I'm not sure that old cottage is big enough for two!"

Mara looked at him inquisitively.

"The pearl diver is back. He suddenly turned up a couple of weeks ago. Maybe he knew you were coming?"

She shook her head. Then a smile crept across her lips as she thought about what the baker had said. Yes, maybe he knew.

T he next morning an elegant woman strolled along the beach. The fishermen greeted her warmly and remembered how, long ago, she had come to them and asked if they usually found pearls here. They chuckled to themselves when they thought about that. But the young woman they knew then as blithe and inquisitive was older now. She had a sad look about her – as if she bore some great sorrow. Had her marriage to the merchant worn her down? And where was her child? Rumour had it that she had given birth. Why wasn't the child with her on her travels? Many of them wanted to ask her questions. But the nets needed to be cleaned of seaweed and fresh sorties lay in front of them, so they let it go.

Mara felt a peculiar tension build up inside as she drew closer to the pearl diver's cottage. She took off her dirty shoes and padded barefoot by the water's edge while she filled her lungs with deep breaths of the sea air.

There was smoke coming from the chimney. He must be at home. Would she and the pearl diver have anything to talk about? Had he found the pearls she had left under the mattress and the book where she'd written down her questions and insights?

2

An old man opened the door when she knocked. He looked skeptically at her for a moment, before his face suddenly softened and she heard him say:

"Are you the pearl diver?"

Mara felt tears begin to well up at this question. She took a step back, tilted her head, as she was in the habit of doing, and said jauntily:

"But it's you who are the pearl diver!"

"Is it?" he asked before he turned and went back into the cottage. He returned quickly with a red cloth pouch that he held out to her. She took it from him.

"I found this under my mattress. Something tells me that it was you who put those pearls there. Is that right?"

She started to laugh; a laughter that bubbled up from a source so pure and joyful that the old man couldn't do anything but laugh himself.

"Yes," she gasped.

"I guessed that," said the pearl diver.

Mara looked at him as he stood there smiling in the doorway. He was slightly bent over; deep cracks in a weather-beaten face; white, relatively thick hair. His whole figure radiated kindness. His eyes had an effect on her; they captivated her. She stepped over the threshold and let her gaze linger on the familiar interior: the table, the spindleback chair, the bed which was made up with the beautiful blue bedspread – its colours somewhat faded now – and the pots and pans on the wall as before, as were the fishing nets by the door.

"The pearls are for you," she said and stroked the red cloth pouch, "to show my gratitude for letting me stay in your cottage when I was young and in need of a place to rest."

"I have no need of so many pearls," said the old man. "But if I may keep just one pearl, to remind me of this moment, I'll place it in the shell I have on the mantelpiece for decoration."

"Did you get it from a mermaid?"

He gave her a little wink and asked her to sit. She devoured the food he offered her – fried fish and boiled vegetables.

"How did you become a pearl diver?" she asked.

"Quite by accident," he said, "it was the same for you, I'd imagine?"

"I found the pearls on the beach. They lay inside mussels that were washed up by the sea right over by the old apple tree. I didn't need to make much of an effort at all."

"Really?"

He looked at this fine figure of a woman as she sat there at his humble table and ate as if she hadn't seen food in days. "If it's so easy to get hold of pearls, why has nobody else in the village found them?"

"Don't you think I've often wondered exactly the same thing?" she replied and motioned with her arms. "Not even the fishermen know the secret!"

"Let me ask you something," said the pearl diver as he leaned over the table towards her. There was a twinkle in his eye:

"Did you have to brave the storm in order to find the pearls?"

Mara nodded.

"Did you have to endure cold before you found them?"

"Actually, I was nearly frozen stiff."

"Did you have to sit patiently and wait for the moon to bless that which came up from the deep?"

Mara looked at the old man in a way which told him that now, for the first time, she really understood the truth about her own secret.

"When you let go of fear and embrace your courage, a pearl is born," the old man said.

They sat in silence. He could see that she was pondering this new insight. Then she said:

"But the old apple tree protected me."

" Oh, yes. That old, crooked apple tree has protected many a forlorn traveller." He leaned back in his chair.

"I myself sought sanctuary by its side when I was on the run."

"What were you running from?"

"From the person I had become."

He cleared his throat.

"Earlier in my life I was a well respected scientist," he said, "but my desire for fame and fortune made me ill. One day while I was sitting working on a speech I was to give at a large conference, I experienced acute head pains. The doctor said it was overwork and told me to have a few weeks rest. After a couple of days in bed, I decided to leave. I didn't know where. I just wanted to get away. I was afraid for my life and felt that I had become someone other than myself."

"I feel the same way now," she said, "I don't know who I am anymore."

"You know well who you are," he protested, "you are a pearl diver. The road ahead is not so much about what to do as how you do it."

"I do not understand."

"Whatever you do, whether you sew or paint or dance or sing or..."

"Weave," she added, and took a sip of water from the mug beside the empty plate.

"That is what you do," he continued. "No matter what that may be, dear pearl diver, the quality of your life and your everyday is much more determined by how you carry out the work you do and how you approach what you do every day. Everyone of us has different talents and we use many of them at different times. No matter what talents you use, give yourself over completely to the task at hand. If it no longer gives you enough satisfaction, find something else to do."

"I was a jeweller when I lived here in the village," she sighed, "but weaving is more suited to my disposition now – even though I've tried to hide it."

"Continue weaving," said the pearl diver, "be happy that you have made a choice about how you want to use your talents."

"Yes, but that's what's so difficult," she protested. "To choose involves saying goodbye over and over again. And that's painful."

"Perhaps," he said, "choice involves both bidding farewell and bidding welcome. You're leaving something, but a pearl diver is also going somewhere."

"How do I know where I'm going to?"

Mara looked up and continued without waiting for an answer: "I tried to do that which I thought was expected of me."

She couldn't stop herself now. On finally meeting this man whom she'd seen in her dreams, the words streamed out of her mouth. She felt as if she could finally speak from her heart to someone who was interested in listening.

"When I lost my child, Helen...," she said the child's name as if she was singing a delicate melody.

"When I lost Helen, I lost a part of myself. The colours disappeared and even though I attempted to find them as I sat at the loom night after night, everything was drab and dreary."

The pearl diver stretched his hand over the table and placed it lightly on the woman's. She wept openly now, sobbing in between. After a while she wiped the tears away with a handkerchief she took from a golden silk pouch that hung from her wrist.

"Please excuse me," she said, "I'm obviously not myself today."

"You are born and reborn every moment my child," said the pearl diver and put another log on the hearth. Mara blew her nose.

"I'm heading for the mountains," she said. "Maybe I'll settle down there and spend my days weaving. But is that enough, do you think? Should I set clearer goals for myself and be sure as to why I want to go to the mountains? It could seem like I'm running away."

The pearl diver sat back down on the spindle back chair.

"If you hear the voice of the mountains in your heart, then move," he said. "You won't need a guide. Just like the ocean brought you here, those mountains have waited patiently for you."

He leaned over the table and stroked her hand gently.

"The most beautiful pearl lies within you. Your life as a pearl diver is all about letting that pearl shine through. Every day. Don't be afraid of your own light."

He inhaled deeply:

"Your sorrow dear Mara, has shaped you and roused you into stepping forward as the person you are. Only those who know what a wound is, can heal."

3

The old man rose from the table and returned with a beautiful, elaborately carved mahogany box, which he opened carefully. Inside it there lay five of the biggest pearls Mara had ever seen.

"These are the most beautiful pearls I have, which I found on different deep-sea dives," he said. "Unlike you, who sat on the beach and watched the mussels wash up at your feet, I had to plunge into the water in order to get hold of mine."

He took out one of the pearls and placed it in Mara's hand.

"Years would often pass between me finding pearls which I thought were of value. I am a very critical man. That's why I go on long journeys in order to curb my nature."

"Where do you go?"

"I wander aimlessly. I play with dolphins, sing with birds or dance with snowflakes. Nature teaches me to live playfully and lightheartedly. If I stay in one place too long, even in my little cottage here," he said, and ran a finger over the tabletop, "then I slip into the same old pattern and start to criticize everyone and everything."

"You criticize?"

She leaned over the table and put the gleaming pearl back in the pearl diver's hand.

"Criticizing other people has been how I've held myself prisoner," he said and peeked down at the box. "These five pearls help me to remember the most important secrets we pearl divers should know and live by."

He chuckled. "You know, wisdom which isn't put into practice has no value."

He took out the little, brown notebook from the drawer under the table.

"I have to admit that I've read this book many times!"

"That was the idea," Mara said, feeling her cheeks redden.

"Lately I've been working on simplifying what I know and then expressing it in its entirety through a simple play on words."

He passed the book to her across the table:

Pearl dive for every day

Pearl. Look for a pearl, or say "thank you" – every day.

Eat. Eat your fear, or play more – every day.

A step is enough. Take one step in the direction of your dreams – every day.

Roses. Roses are best when given away, to yourself or others – every day.

Love. Love what you do or find something to love in what you do – every day.

"It's like a recipe," she said. "A recipe for how I can make every day shine."

She pointed to one of the letters:

"What do you mean when you say I should eat my own fear?"

"Eating is about digesting what you take in. Some of it gets flushed out of the system and some of it remains to nourish the soul."

He sighed. "Eating my own criticism has been about distinguishing sound skepticality from judging. You know, even the biggest flaw has its good sides."

"Even fear?"

Mara closed her eyes and visualised a large, black surface dissected by a thin line. Someone was walking along the line; a small dot moving far away. A person: a tiny person.

"I fear that I'll never be truly loved," she said and opened up her eyes quickly again. "I'm afraid that if I show myself as I really am, then no man could love me."

The pearl diver leaned back and laughed so hard he nearly fell off the little spindle back chair.

"That's one of the most stupid things I've heard in a long time," he gasped when he'd finally stopped laughing. "It's incredible what fear can make people believe!"

"Well what if it's true? What if my talents make a man feel inferior? I've already experienced that once."

"If you conceal your talents or allow them to lie unused, then you can never grow and mature as a pearl diver. Instead, you're using all your everyday energy to hide who you are."

Mara let the old man's words sink in.

"My daughter Helen tried to say exactly the same thing to me when she was alive – although she couldn't express it the way you do. She said that I should enjoy the colours in every moment."

The two pearl divers sat in silence for a long time, both lost in their own history. A storm was brewing. The shutters outside the window began to rattle. Mara felt that it was time to put down these heavy thoughts amongst the stones and mussels on the beach.

"It seems the sea knows that you've arrived," said the old man at last.

"Yes," she replied. "Tonight I must sing my songs in the shelter of the old apple tree."

4

She found it difficult to see in front of her. The sand whipped her cheeks and blew into the eyes. But Mara knew this place well and before long she could make out the contour of the old apple tree. She greeted it with a kiss, before lying down at the trunk as she had done before - digging her hands into the sand. The branches protected her from the worst of the wind. Even though she was freezing and her teeth chattered, she felt like the cold caressed her in a strange way.

The storm raged, Mara sang her lament to the sea. All she wanted to say, and that which could not be put into words, lay in this night song: her sorrow for the child that was taken from her; her anger over the hard blows she'd suffered - time and time again; her failed marriage; her fear of the future... Mara let out a wail - like a primal sound from the dawn of time; a prayer: "*Oh, master weaver, keep my heart alive, so my wounds and scars may heal and my life be blessed with pearls...*"

The woman's song gave life to the old apple tree by the sea. At first it swayed, as if it wanted to tear itself up by the roots. Then it stopped moving and remained quite still. Was it waiting for something? A tall, long-limbed woman with golden hair glided graciously out of the trunk, a bit hesitantly at first. She held another person by the hand - a dark, buxom woman with a voluptuous form, stepped out onto the beach after her. She, in turn, led a younger, radiant, slightly cross-eyed man from the trunk of the tree. He held the hand of a beautiful little American Indian boy.

And that's how it came to pass: from this old apple tree several hundred people stepped out onto the beach. In different colours and shapes, in swaying, dancing steps, they circled hand-in-hand - like a strong, dignifying ring - around Mara.

This song united them:

> *Pearl diver:*
> *You are not alone!*
> *As the stars glitter in the weave of the night,*
> *Your pearl shines in our eyes.*
> *See your strength in our faces!*
> *Feel your warmth in our hands!*
> *Hear your voice in our song!*
> *Pearl diver:*
> *Become what you are...*

5

When Mara awoke she no longer laid under the apple tree, but under the blue bedspread in the old pearl diver's cottage. He was beside the bed, watching over her.

"You have a fever," he said. "I thought it would be best if you stayed in the house tonight. You are hard on yourself".

She drank the sweet warm drink he handed her.

"The baker and the jeweller were here this morning. They wondered where you had got to. I told them you had fallen ill and that you could stay here until you felt better, if you so wished."

She nodded, handed him back the cup and let her head sink into the pillow. "What do you mean by saying that I'm hard on myself? After all, isn't that how one reaches one's goals and becomes the best version of oneself?"

"Is it?"

A cool wind blew through the little window over the bed. A shiver went through her body.

"For a long time, I believed that if I worked hard I'd reach my goals," he said. "And, of course I still believe that."

He straightened up in the chair.

"But I've also found out that for pearl divers like us, there is another insight."

"Which is?"

"The law of transformation."

"Perhaps it's the fever but I don't quite follow," said Mara and gave a faint smile.

The pearl diver looked at her and continued:

"For a long time, I was one of those who believed that being successful was about having as much control as possible. I had big ambitions and I pursued them with a vengeance. As time went on and I achieved my goals, I discovered I couldn't manage to enjoy either the success or my life."

"You don't set goals for yourself anymore?"

"But of course. An old pearl diver is always true to his ambitions. But there's one big difference from before... "

He tucked the blanket tighter around her. "I surrender myself more to life and to every passing moment, if that's not too philosophical," he said and winked at her. "I do my best every day and then I let chance do the rest."

Mara swallowed. Her gaze drifted from the old man's face over to the mantelpiece where the little shell lay which held the pearl she'd given him.

"You mean that if something still doesn't work after you've given it your best shot, then it just wasn't meant to be?"

"Yes," he answered. "And I think that something else will turn up that is better suited to me and to my talents. Instead of criticizing others and bemoaning their lack of effort and inability to get something done, I now allow myself, to a greater extent, to look for the good feeling in every moment. Thus I bring along joy, instead of demanding it from others. Now, I use more playful energy to get things done, instead of pointing out lack of progress to everyone."

"Like a dolphin?"

"Yes, like a dolphin," repeated the pearl diver as he gave a slight smile. "I don't let the goal out of my sight, but I relax more and rely on that which is to develop doing so in it's own time and to it's own rhythm. I've realized that I can't force a butterfly to learn to fly!"

Mara listened to the old man's voice. It had such a beautiful ring to it and what he said touched her heart and made her think of what she'd experienced at night under the apple tree. She drifted slowly off to sleep while the old pearl diver held her hand and told her a story, as one would tell a child:

"Once upon a time there was a little angel who was looking forward to getting started on his deeds amongst the people on earth. For a long time he'd looked down from the cloud where he hid and saw that people were in need of good deeds. Together with some other angels he went on his first trip to earth. But no matter what he did or which good work he tried to carry out, there wasn't one single person on earth who noticed. Indeed, they went so far as to deny the existence of angels on earth. The little angel was beginning to get very tired. One afternoon, he saved a man from drowning, helped an old woman think good thoughts and held his hand over a business to stop it going bankrupt – all without a word of thanks, not so much as a glance in his direction. Well, the little angel sat down and started to cry. His tears ran like beautiful, white bubbles down into the depths of the ocean. A couple of mussels noticed these pearls of light from above. They had never seen anything like it. They opened themselves up and received the pure light coming towards them, then concealed the angel tears in their hearts."

The pearl diver pulled the blue bedspread up to better cover Mara.

"And we pearl divers have known since then, that when we find a pearl in a mussel, we've found an angel tear. Then we should turn our hearts to the angels that watch over us everyday and give thanks."

Part 4

When a carpet reveals the hidden door,
a pearl is born.

1

Mara wasn't young anymore. Faint wrinkles were visible in her narrow face, but the hair that fell in curls around it was still a beautiful, golden colour. She liked to wear it loose when she sat and weaved.

Mara stretched out and absorbed the comfort of the warm room. It was neat and simply furnished with a few of her tapestries as decoration on the walls and floor. She had weaved throughout the night, as she usually did when she was taking great pains with a piece. A slight movement of the hand to divide the warp and insert the weft and a new silver thread appeared in the gloom. She didn't need daylight in order to weave. She was gifted with an innate adroitness. She held the pictures inside like small secrets and the strokes came through a rhythmic dance with the weave itself.

Some said that her tapestries had healing properties. A variety of people, with different ailments, had lain or sat upon them and declared themselves healthy due to the energy from the patterns and motifs within. Others said that the tapestries had led them to venture more and give themselves a new chance.

Mara slowly got up from the loom and opened the front door. She leaned against the doorframe and gazed out at the patchy yellow-green mosaic of meadows and fields that stretched up toward the high mountains and lay in the twilight this early morning. A rainbow kissed the landscape to new life and she thought about an old pearl diver insight she guarded in her heart.

The courtyard was full of people and the carpet merchant's servant shot her a quick glance before he started talking to a couple of men who had a cartload of carpets from different cities and lands with them. She remained standing, perplexed over her next course of action, wondering what to do with the carpet she'd weaved, when she heard a voice behind her:

"Are you the one who weaves tapestries of such beauty that people find God when they look at them?"

Mara turned around. A man stood there, neither young nor old, but some years younger than herself. His hair was a touch grey above the ears even though it was dark and close-cropped. He was fresh-faced and there was something about his round head, big nose and the way his mouth turned slightly downwards when he smiled, that reminded her of the old carpet merchant.

"Every tapestry has a life of its own," she answered and suddenly she understood who he was.

"Simon, the carpet merchant's prodigal son," he said and offered her his hand. "I've ordered a magic carpet," he said. "Can it fly?"

"You'll have to ask it," said Mara, suddenly feeling embarrassed. She could see that her answer aroused his interest. Something in his eyes lit up, a glimmer, a deeper curiosity. He lifted the tapestry out of the cart, spread it out carefully on the cobblestones in the courtyard and studied it.

"I see a man and a woman," he said pensively after a short pause. "They're adorned in birds' feathers. He's a radiant, turquoise colour – like a peacock – and she's a deeper red. I see the ocean surging along a beach and mountains that..."

He stopped himself. She knew what he saw. Because there, on the cobblestones in the courtyard, Simon saw the story of his life right up to this moment: childhood games, the halcyon nights and days of youth, the ravages of the war and all the beautiful women he'd left his mark upon and since turned away from. He saw things he'd never told another living soul, like the time he saved his father's life and stopped his brother from killing a rival.

Simon looked up, but now it was he who was embarrassed. He looked down and said: "This carpet shall be given a place of pride in my room."

Without another word he rolled the carpet up and with a powerful jerk, hefted it up onto his shoulder. He bid her farewell and went into one of the buildings.

2

The third week after their first meeting, Simon knocked on the door of the house where she lived. Mara had seen his figure approaching from where she stood in her usual spot - in the doorway, ready to greet the morning. It surprised her that he didn't ride, as his father usually did, but went on foot like a wayfarer. He was sweaty and covered with dust when he greeted her. She offered him a cold drink and bade him sit on a bench outside the house in the shadow of an old apple tree, where there stood a little table with a flower vase upon it.

"It's going to be a warm day," he said, as if saying something for the sake of it.

They inspected each other. Something about this man made her feel assured and happy. His characteristic mouth broke into a cheerful smile. She sat down beside him on the bench and poured some water with a dash of peppermint into their glasses.

"What's the secret," he asked, after he'd quenched his thirst. "How do you make a tapestry come alive?"

"What do you mean?"

"When I looked at the carpet you gave me, I caught glimpses of my entire life, even things that I've never told another living soul about! How do you do it?"

"It's not me. It's you," she said slowly.

"That's not true," he said, becoming impatient. "I've seen many tapestries, but I've never been so captivated."

"Every tapestry bears its destiny," she said and sipped some water from the glass before placing it back on the table. "Your tapestry bears your destiny. If you manage to love your destiny, the tapestry comes to life."

Simon looked at Mara where she sat on the bench, speaking in her calm, gentle manner. She was wearing a bluish grey dress and her abundant hair fell about her shoulders. Her eyes were like a dark blue ocean he could sink into, and he sensed in some strange way that he had finally come home. On all his travels, among all his women, he had been searching for this one woman. She was the meaning of his search and she was what he needed to find happiness again.

"To weave is to walk step-by-step along the path of beauty," she went on, stealing a glance at him, her eye contact sending a warm shudder through him.

"The most difficult thing for a weaver is not to get ahead in the world. Her voice glowed with passion now. "The art is rather to weave every moment of your life equal to the dreams in your minds eye."

As she reached for the glass on the table, he took hold of her slender hand and brought it slowly to his lips.

3

M ara felt attracted to Simon. Not by power or strength, but by virtue of his personality, that alluring, irresistible and immortal personality – the dreamer whose dreams come true. His fingers glided softly along her shoulder and arm. A puff of wind rustled the old apple tree that stood guard by the house. It dawned upon her that it was the same wind that, on a night long ago, had blown his scent close to her face. She had loved him long before she knew he existed.

"Come," she said, "let's take a walk in the woods."

They wandered through early summer's freshly blossomed world. The lilies of the valley's time was past; they had faded and disappeared. Starflowers were now in bloom throughout the forest. The veil of small star-shaped flowers blossomed around the old, twisted tree roots smooth and perfectly still as a milk-white mist. And by the side of the path, sunbeams played in floating pearl-grey spider's webs woven over blades of grass and twigs.

After a while, he stopped, turned towards her and gently placed his hands around her shoulders.

"I love you," he said.

She looked at him solemnly before she said, "How can you say such a thing to an older woman?"

"Love wants it that way," he said.

She bent down to pick up two fragments of a speckled bird eggshell that lay on the path, and tried to fit them together again.

"I am too old to give you children," she said. "The child I gave birth to died long ago."

She held the brittle bird shells in the palm of her hand as they walked on together in silence.

"Love is itself a child," he said, after a time, while he tried to find words for what he had on his mind. "Of course, a man wants to have children with the woman he loves. But when that's not possible, he must listen for the signs that love weaves. My bloodline will live on with my sister's children."

They reached the edge of the forest. The high mountains could be seen in the distance.

"It's a sacrifice you're offering," she said and sighed.

"A sacrifice is also a gift; just as gold, myrrh and frankincense are gifts."

"The most precious you have."

"Sacrifice or gift. Love is about giving and receiving," he said. "The one who sacrifices something doesn't necessarily loose something. Perhaps he discovers something else, something quite different from what he'd imagined."

She threw the eggshells away and touched his hand gently.

"In a way, I'm hardly a woman, since I cannot bear you a child. A woman's lot is to give birth."

"You judge yourself harshly," he said. "You are born and reborn every moment."

He put his arm on her shoulder in a way that seemed both protective and loving. Simon's words called something to mind; the old pearl diver had said the same thing to her. It consoled her and made her smile.

"There are many children who've never known their mothers," Simon went on, "if you want to be a mother and I a father then we can adopt an orphaned child."

He noticed how Mara's body finally relaxed. She leaned against him and let him hold her. He could feel the form of her body. He became conscious of the weight of her head on his arm, the curve of her hips against his own, the locks of her hair which tickled his neck and the light dress which was nearly as delicate as her skin. Desire rose in a powerful and compelling warm wave. The air in his lungs got stuck. He pulled her closer.

"I've been waiting for you every day and longing for you on all my travels," he whispered.

His warmth and weight enveloped her like a blanket. She closed her eyes and felt how his mouth found its way to her lips and opened them. Ah, if she could only stretch this moment out to the end of her days!

Slowly, almost clumsily due to the trembling of his hands, Simon opened the button that fastened the back pocket on his trousers. He took out a beautiful, old gold ring adorned with two red rubies and a sparkling white pearl. "Will you wear this ring as a symbol of my love for you?"

Mara recognized the ring immediately. In astonishment, she let him put it on the middle finger of her left hand.

"Now you interpret the symbols," he said.

"Two hearts and one dream," she answered, her lips seeking his.

4

It didn't go unnoticed that Simon had put a ring on Mara's finger. The outside world observed what happened and made it their business. It took a few months before the rumours reached Mara's ears but one day she heard what they were talking about behind her back: "He's a crook. He's been cheating on all his trips. A former business associate has proof."

That evening, Simon didn't come to see her as usual, and when he didn't turn up the next evening either, she went and knocked on the door of the carpet merchant's house. There she was told that he'd been charged with fraud and taken to the prison in the city, a day's ride from the village. Mara guessed who was behind these terrible charges but said nothing. As she made her way back to the house and the loom, she could feel a tightening in her chest which reminded her of her previous life when she still lived in the big house amidst the noise and racket of the city. Was this how he would avenge himself; the man whom she had once given so many of her pearls?

Was he still rummaging in that ditch? Had the darkness such a hold on him that he made false accusations in order to get his way?

She let out a heavy sigh as she opened the door to the little cottage. Tonight her loom would be her prayer chamber.

Simon was behind bars in one of the innermost dungeons. His contact with the outside world over the next few days consisted of a few whispered words from the guard who brought him bread and water and some recurrent noises. He knew when they changed the watch, he counted the vehicles that came in and out of the yard and he listened carefully to try to identify voices and footsteps distorted by distance. He tried to sleep to make time pass quickly, but inactivity and apprehension drove sleep away. A shorter man would have been able to stretch out fully on the bunk, but for Simon the bed was like a strait jacket.

He was dizzy and his thoughts revolved around Mara. What kind of story had she heard about why he'd been put behind lock and key? What must she think of him? He knew that he was innocent and the accusations against him were false and malicious but how could she know that?

The lice in the mattress settled in his scalp and multiplied quickly. They caused his armpits to itch and made him scratch until he bled. He tried to stay calm. He tried to walk around in a circle to avoid cramp and to get his muscles working, but it was difficult to stand up straight as his head banged against the ceiling.

After a few days he was moved to a slightly larger cell. Every morning and afternoon he was taken out to work in the forge. Even though it was noisy and hot, he relished the chance to be physically active, and he actually liked getting to know this craft.

Simon had been gone for weeks. Mara didn't know if he was alive or dead, she only knew that she had to continue weaving to keep her spirits up. After a while she became aware of an emptiness that caused more anxiety as the days wore on and she still hadn't heard from him. She tried to find out what exactly he was charged with, and the rumours were unambiguous: Simon had been engaged in extensive fraudulent business activities involving carpets, tapestries, art and gold and was now awaiting his well-deserved punishment. In addition, he'd killed a man who had tried to expose his dealings.

The moon rose, and the sky between it and the mountains looked as if it was sprinkled with gold dust. That night as she stared at the tapestry she was making, she had a dreamlike vision of a woman wandering alone through a beautiful forest. She came to a lake. At the edge of the water, there was a little cottage. She went into it and looked around. Although it was still quite bright outside and the curtains were drawn back, there was a gas lamp burning. A fire in the hearth cast a beautiful glimmer over a slightly worn carpet. A table in the middle of the room was covered with a white tablecloth.

She went further in and came to a small bedroom. The smell of freshly plucked violets met her as she came through the doorway. To her surprise she saw that the wall was covered in runic symbols and old inscriptions from texts and languages which people no longer speak. The symbols changed constantly as she stared at them.

A four-poster bed stood in the middle of the room, a bluish-green curtain ran along four sides. She sensed that Simon was there, behind the curtain. She called his name but no one answered. Then she approached the bed and drew the curtain slowly aside. He wasn't there, only a resounding empty echo. Her eyes fell upon an old, black key which lay upon the white silk pillow. She picked up the key, felt its weight and pressed it hard into her warm palm.

Mara didn't know how long she'd been staring into the tapestry. She thought she'd been crying but her eyes were dry. Finally she fell into a sudden and deep sleep. She awoke by the cold morning air streaming in through the open window and it brought with it the noise of a carriage that stopped in front of the door. The old, stooped-over servant, the servant she met when she'd delivered the tapestry to Simon knocked at the door.

"I just want to tell you that Simon is alive and misses you," he said, his eyes darting nervously about.

"Can you get me two horses?" she asked. The voice wasn't her own; it came from a deep place within.

He seemed hesitant at first but she smiled in such a friendly way and caught his eye, so the old man nodded pensively and with a deep bow, took his leave of her.

For six days and six nights Mara sat by the loom. When the dew lay on the ground on the seventh morning, she pulled on some men's clothing - black travelling attire - that fitted her well. Her rosy, red lips smiled calmly and encouragingly at the reflection in the mirror.

Not long after, a dark figure rode through a wet forest with a bundle across the horse's flank. The wood pigeons cooed intimately in the high trees as she rode under them. The sparrows sang in the drizzle. A fox came out of the thicket along the path. It stopped short and looked at the rider, its tail lowered. Then it glided past her like a red flame and was extinguished in the wet grass of the forest floor.

"The animals and birds in the forest are happy with the earth as it is," she thought. "Shouldn't the earth be sufficient for the children of men too? Why are kings and politicians and businessmen so filled with greed? Why do they need to fabricate charges and throw people into prison to hold sway over the fate of others? Is there no leader who can come to an agreement with himself and say: Love is my guide and dignity my friend!"

She rode out of the woods and set off at a gallop over a field dotted with overgrown thorn bushes. Two ravens, who'd been taking a dignified stroll in the short grass, flew quickly away as the rider tore by. The air was filled with promise, and she gazed out over meadows and fields. Far away, at the end of the plain, she saw the tower of the prison where Simon was being kept. Its stark silhouette rose up toward the sky.

5

Simon kneeled in his cold and dark cell. He bowed down in the light of a solitary tallow candle and said his evening prayers on the little prayer mat that had been tossed to him at vespers. The night was pitch-black as usual, and yet it was no longer a heavy darkness. For the first time since he had been put in prison, the darkness was pregnant with hope.

"A stranger asked me to give you this carpet," said the guard who came with food and drink. "So you could begin to pray again."

The guard laughed heartily as he tossed the carpet into the cell.

While Simon lay there and felt the echo of hopes and dreams that his love's prayer mat brought about in him, he listened to the silence of the cold room. He couldn't see Mara's form, but he felt a female presence through the mat she had weaved – warp interlaced in weft. It spoke to him of pattern and shape. It spoke to him of how paths in life can be difficult to understand, but that they have their meaning and fulfil their task.

"Do not try to separate the threads of the weave from one another," the carpet said. "Life and death, happiness and unhappiness, past and present are joined together – like two lovers. And yet there is a pattern in these threads, which can be found by those who have a tender gaze."

Simon took the little tallow candle, got down on his knees once more and turned to look at the carpet. He remained kneeling for a long time and gazed at it in silence. He saw a boat sailing in calm water with the wind behind it. He, himself, stood astern and held the rudder. At the bow there sat a beautiful, naked woman trailing her fingers in the water. Under the boat there swam a great fish in the dark blue shadow of the keel. And in the middle of the fish's belly he saw something that looked like the outline of a key. He looked closer. Yes, the fish had a key in its stomach, a big, black key. What kind of key could it be? Simon took a deep breath. Where had he seen such a key? In the hand of the prison guard! It hung from his belt!

The forge was scorching hot and filthy. His body glistened with sweat. Simon struck the red-hot iron and shaped it after the imprint the carpet had shown him. He moved slowly so as not to arouse interest and pretended to busy himself with a wheel frame. He mustn't look too eager. It took a long time before the key lay red-hot and fully formed in front of him. He swayed for a moment, his upper body moved in confused, small circles. With difficulty, like a very old person, he studied the room carefully. There was a door not far from where he stood; a side door in the very prison wall itself, with a stone staircase down to the fields that surrounded the entire town. It was this door that the key fitted. He knew that. Sometimes it was barely watched. In a while it would be the changing of the guards. The key would have cooled down and they would be busy with the food trolley. That was his chance. Now it was just a matter of waiting and working.

At vespers all the guards' attention was focused on the food trolley. At the right moment, Simon stood in front of the door. His hand quivered as he put the key in the lock and he turned it around with such force and presence of mind that even he was surprised. He knew he didn't have much time. Silently he snuck out and ran as fast as he could down the stairs and on. A twig snapped under the weight of his foot. The hill down towards the fields and meadows was moist and slippery. If he could only manage to reach the cover of the forest before they discovered he was gone, he'd have a chance!

He ran through a field of barley. The grain grew poorly but the whole field was packed with oxbow daisies. They looked like the moon was reflected in them as in a beautiful tiny lake. He jumped over a fence, ran over a small bridge and then through more fields. A star hung in the sky, twinkling like a greeting from a night long ago.

Suddenly the dense forest enveloped him in a deep darkness that hung in the very trees and branches. It was overwhelming. A black wing whizzed by his cheek. A bat. He shivered as he ran, his heart thumped like a mechanical clock in his chest. He was counting on the help of his well-honed sense of direction to find his way to his own village without too many detours. But he soon realized that it wasn't easy as he had to stay hidden from the road at all times.

He stopped now and again, sure that he had lost his way, only to continue determinedly. Simon was worn out from his time in prison and couldn't run much more. But the knowledge that Mara waited for him, spurred him on. He wiped the sweat from his forehead and went on, pushing his muscles to the utmost. Finally he heard the sound of a brook, an insignificant tributary, but he knew that this brook ran alongside an old, partially overgrown road that would lead him to her house – eventually.

6

Mara listened to the silence of the landscape and thought she perceived a peculiar tone behind the early morning chirping of the birds. Was he on his way? She saddled both horses to be on the safe side. Afterwards she stood in the doorway as usual and watched the sky light up. Alongside the garden, just beyond the old apple tree, there lay a wheat field. Two roe deer stood there now, and in the twilight they looked rose-red against all the grains. She let her gaze wander out over the fields and up towards the mountains. It seemed to her that she could converse with the landscape that surrounded her, as if with her own foremother.

"Will I, for once in my life, experience following the flame of my passion?" she whispered. The dew-kissed rose petals responded with a cool fragrance from the high hedge that clung to the house and wreathed the windows. The sun rose into sight over the mountain range at the same moment. Its radiance gave the magnificent, peaceful landscape an unexpected manifold of life and a new palette. The dew upon the grass gleamed with countless small diamonds.

And there, like a staggering central character on an open stage, Simon stumbled out of the edge of the forest. His face, hair and worn out clothes were grimy with sweat and dust. He stopped in his tracks when he saw her and held his hand over his eyes:

"They're after me," he shouted. "They'll soon be here."

"The horses are saddled with all the provisions we need," she said and rose quickly from the bench. "I'll go with you."

He kissed her passionately before he drank greedily of the water she gave him, and poured the rest over his head.

"We must make for the sea! We'll find a ship there we can board."

Mara ran quickly into the house and came out with a beautiful, woven, dark blue shirt. Five pearls served as buttons on its collar.

"From one pearl diver to another," she said mysteriously. "Put it on, it's for you. It'll bring us luck on the journey."

He pulled the shirt over his head unsteadily and fastened a leather belt around his waist. His weary body no longer able to discern time; it seemed to him that he found himself in the midst of eternity, a short time later, they rode as fast as they could – westward toward the sea.

The mountains lay behind them. The forest around them opened up. Oak and maple were gradually replaced by thin, crooked birch. The woodland track they rode upon was no longer a road but a narrow sandy path. In front of them there lay a row of dunes of differing heights. They rode up to the top of them and found the sea right ahead of them. Simon stopped his horse and looked out over it, as did Mara. They dismounted and held tightly around each other while they felt the fresh salty sea air on their faces.

Simon took a deep breath. He hadn't been near a beach for a long time, and the air, so saturated with the smell of seaweed, healed his weary limbs. He thought about the ships that for centuries had glided out from this coast to all corners of the world. He thought about how he now was about to leave his village and his people in order to find a ship that would sail himself and his woman to a new beginning. Many conflicting emotions crowded his mind. Now at this parting moment, this landscape was more precious to him than ever, made so solemn and so strangely beautified by his imminent departure.

Simon grasped Mara's hand and squeezed it. Her deep, clear eyes welled with tears. The beach stretched out on both sides of them, as far as the eye could see, bone-white and scattered with pebbles and mussels. Everything was desolate and naked in a noble way – like the beginning or the end of an ardent adventure.

"Look! Over there!"

Mara half ran and half jumped across the beach with the horse in tow, before she stopped by an old ramshackle cottage. It seemed uninhabited, but she found a small key under one of the stones in the doorstep and went in.

"Come," she said and grabbed Simon's hand. "This is the pearl diver's cottage. I lived here when I was young."

"Did you live together with a pearl diver?"

"In a way, yes."

He looked at her in wonder, sensing a joyous elation right in the middle of all the anxiety about their current situation and the forthcoming journey.

"A long time ago there lived a pearl diver here. I only met him in person once."

She ran her fingers through her hair. "He helped me to dive deeper than I thought I could."

Simon nodded, asked her to go on, but she stopped herself. "I'll tell you more some other time," she said and walked over to the table. She pulled out a little drawer and peeped inside. The note book was no longer there but she found a yellowed scrap of paper under a beautiful brownish-white conch.

"That's your handwriting," said Simon, as she took it out. "Did you write that?"

Mara nodded. In the faint light that came through the little cottage window, they read it together:

Your talents are like seeds hidden in a mussel.
Turn them into pearls by mindful action every day!
Then count your blessings!

Epilogue

Pearldive

You asked for strength.
What you got was hardship to endure
- to become strong.

You asked for wisdom.
What you got were problems to solve
– to become wise.

You asked for love.
What you got were people to care for
– to become love.

You asked for guidance.
What you got were opportunities to choose between
 – to become a guide.

You asked for success.
What you got were talents to use
– to become more of you.

You asked for peace.
What you got were wounds to heal
– to walk in peace.